MEET THE
CHAMPIONS

DK | Penguin Random House

For DK

Editors Vicky Armstrong, Clare Millar
Designers David McDonald, Mark Penfound
Production Designer Wil Cruz
Pre-Production Producer Kavita Varma
Senior Producer Lloyd Robertson
Managing Editor Sarah Harland
Design Manager Guy Harvey
Publisher Julie Ferris
Art Director Lisa Lanzarini
Publisher Director Simon Beecroft

Reading Consultant Linda B. Gambrell, Ph.D.

For WWE

Global Publishing Manager Steve Pantaleo
Photo Department Frank Vitucci,
Josh Tottenham, Jamie Nelson,
Mike Moran, JD Sestito, Melissa Halladay,
Lea Girard
Legal Lauren Dienes-Middlen

First American Edition, 2019
Published in the United States by DK Publishing
1450 Broadway, Suite 801, New York, New York 10018
DK, a Division of Penguin Random House LLC

Previously published as three separate titles:
DK Reader Level 2 WWE The Rock (2014),
DK Reader Level 2 WWE John Cena (2014),
DK Reader Level 2 WWE Sheamus (2014)

Page design copyright ©2019 Dorling Kindersley Limited

14 15 16 10 9 8 7 6 5 4 3 2 1
002-316425-July/2019

A catalog record for this book is available from
the Library of Congress.

ISBN: 978-1-4654-9037-7 (Paperback)
ISBN: 978-1-4654-9046-9 (Hardback)

DK books are available at special discounts when purchased
in bulk for sales promotions, premiums, fund-raising,
or educational use. For details, contact: DK Publishing Special
Markets, 1450 Broadway, Suite 801, New York, New York 10018
SpecialSales@dk.com

Printed and bound in China

A WORLD OF IDEAS:
SEE ALL THERE IS TO KNOW

www.wwe.com
www.dk.com

Contents

A LEVEL FOR EVERY READER

This book is a part of an exciting four-level reading series to support children in developing the habit of reading widely for both pleasure and information. Each book is designed to develop a child's reading skills, fluency, grammar awareness, and comprehension in order to build confidence and enjoyment when reading.

Ready for a Level 2 (Beginning to Read) book

A child should:

- be able to recognize a bank of common words quickly and be able to blend sounds together to make some words.
- be familiar with using beginner letter sounds and context clues to figure out unfamiliar words.
- sometimes correct his/her reading if it doesn't look right or make sense.
- be aware of the need for a slight pause at commas and a longer one at periods.

A valuable and shared reading experience

For many children, reading requires much effort, but adult participation can make reading both fun and easier. Here are a few tips on how to use this book with a young reader:

Check out the contents together:

- read about the book on the back cover and talk about the contents page to help heighten interest and expectation.
- discuss new or difficult words.
- chat about labels, annotations, and pictures.

Support the reader:

- give the book to the young reader to turn the pages.
- where necessary, encourage longer words to be broken into syllables, sound out each one, and then flow the syllables together; ask him/her to reread the sentence to check the meaning.
- encourage the reader to vary her/his voice as she/he reads; demonstrate how to do this if helpful.

Talk at the end of each book, or after every few pages:

- ask questions about the text and the meaning of the words used—this helps develop comprehension skills.
- read the glossary at the end of the book and encourage the reader to learn the words and their definitions.

Series consultant, Dr. Linda Gambrell, Distinguished Professor of Education at Clemson University, has served as President of the National Reading Conference, the College Reading Association, and the International Reading Association.

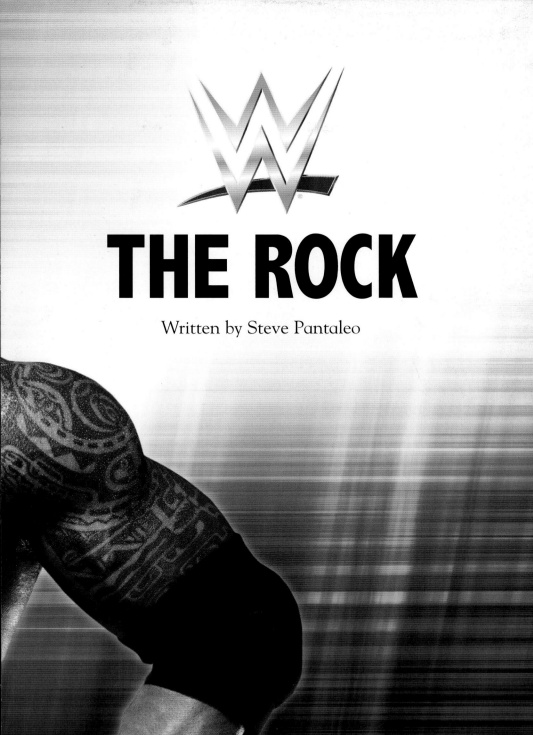

THE ROCK

Written by Steve Pantaleo

The Rock is the most electrifying
man in all of entertainment.
He is also the most charismatic
Superstar in WWE history.
Born Dwayne Johnson, The Rock
is an eight-time WWE Champion
and a Hollywood sensation.
Descending from the legendary
Anoa'i family, The Rock seemed
destined for greatness.

Both his father and grandfather were Superstars before him, making him WWE's first third-generation Superstar. However, The Rock needed unlimited grit and willpower to achieve his amazing success.

The Rock Stats

Height: 6' 5"

Weight: 260 lbs.

Hometown: Miami, Florida

Signature Moves: Rock Bottom, People's Elbow

Long before becoming a WWE Superstar, Dwayne Johnson was a standout football player. In college, he played for the Miami Hurricanes and was part of the 1991 National Championship team. He excelled in football, but his heart was set on another goal, one that was in his blood: WWE.

Dwayne Johnson's father, Rocky Johnson, trained him rigorously.

Rocky Johnson

He wanted his son to know exactly how tough life in the ring could be. Choosing to honor his father and grandfather, the budding star debuted in WWE as Rocky Maivia. This combined his father's name with that of his grandfather, High Chief Peter Maivia.

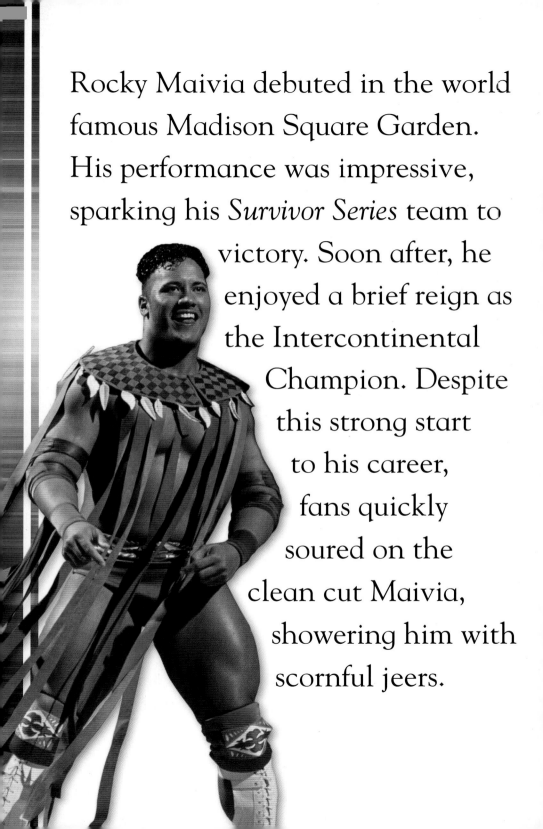

Rocky Maivia debuted in the world famous Madison Square Garden. His performance was impressive, sparking his *Survivor Series* team to victory. Soon after, he enjoyed a brief reign as the Intercontinental Champion. Despite this strong start to his career, fans quickly soured on the clean cut Maivia, showering him with scornful jeers.

The Rock's Electrifying MSG Moments

***Survivor Series* 1996:** Rocky Maivia dominates in his debut match.

***Royal Rumble* 2000:** The Rock wins the 30-man *Royal Rumble* Match.

***WrestleMania XX, 2004:** The Rock n' Sock Connection reunites.

***Survivor Series* 2011:** Fans chant, "You still got it!" in his return match, recognizing that The Rock had not lost a step.

Maivia did not let the hostile crowds discourage him. Instead, he joined the villainous Nation of Domination and quickly unseated Faarooq as the group's leader. This bold new attitude propelled him to a long-lasting reign as the Intercontinental Champion.

Now known as The Rock, he led The Nation against rivals D-Generation X and Stone Cold Steve Austin.

DX's Triple H beat him for the Intercontinental Title at *SummerSlam* 1998, but The Rock's momentum was still building.

The WWE brass knew The Rock
had the spirit of a champion.
Little did the WWE Universe
know, The People's Champion was
already aligned with WWE boss
Mr. McMahon. This secret was
revealed when he won his first
WWE Championship in a 14-man
tournament at *Survivor Series* 1998.

As The Corporate Champion, The Rock had some of the most intense battles in history with rival Mankind. He also headlined *WrestleMania* for the first time, colliding with Stone Cold Steve Austin.

"Rock Bottom"

Over time, fans became drawn to The Rock's magnetic personality. His interviews were so entertaining that crowds had no choice but to cheer him. As his popularity soared, he shed ties with the McMahons and fought for the people.

He even embraced Mankind, forming the Rock 'n' Sock Connection. Known for their memorable comedic timing, the unlikely duo also clicked in the ring. They won

three World Tag Team Championships before The Rock went solo. Soon after, The Brahma Bull won the 2000 *Royal Rumble* and eventually defeated Triple H for the WWE Championship. The Rock's career skyrocketed.

The Rock Says…

"Know your role and shut your mouth!"
"If you smell what The Rock is cookin'!"
"It doesn't matter what your name is!"
"I will layeth the smacketh down!"
"Finally… The Rock has come back!"
"You will go one-on-one with the Great One!"
"Just bring it!"
"The millions (AND MILLIONS!)
   of The Rock's fans…"

During this dramatic rise, The Rock pinned Kurt Angle for his sixth WWE Championship, punching his ticket to *WrestleMania X-7*. On WWE's grandest stage, he suffered his most crushing loss when Stone Cold defeated him with assistance from Mr. McMahon.

However, The Great One would not be down for long. He helped save WWE from a hostile takeover in 2001 by winning the WCW Championship from Booker T. Later, he led Team WWE to victory against the WCW/ECW Alliance, crushing the invasion.

In February 2002, The Rock challenged the immortal Hulk Hogan to go one-on-one at *WrestleMania X8*. The match would feature the most legendary Superstars from two different eras competing against each other. Only in WWE can two generations collide in one epic encounter.

When the two icons stared each other down, the crowd went wild,  alternating chants for both The Rock and The Hulkster.

No one was sitting. Feeding off his Hulkamaniacs, Hogan punished The Rock with a Big Boot and patented Leg Drop. However, The Rock recovered to hit a Rock Bottom and win the historic match.

The two competitors showed proper respect by shaking hands after the match. The win boosted The Rock toward another title opportunity at *Vengeance* 2002. There, he beat both Kurt Angle and Undertaker for his record-setting seventh WWE Championship.

The Rock had nearly accomplished everything he could in the ring. So, he broadened his horizons, starring in movies. He also showcased his musical talent, performing humorous "Rock concerts" for WWE crowds. Still, one goal had eluded him: defeating Stone Cold Steve Austin at *WrestleMania*.

In two previous attempts, he failed to defeat his most bitter rival on the grandest stage. *WrestleMania XIX* would be his last chance. He needed this win to cement his legacy, but Austin was tough as nails. The encounter was fierce. Both Superstars used several finishing moves hoping to end the match, but neither would give up. It took an astounding three Rock Bottoms to keep Stone Cold down for the three-count, but The Rock had done it. He notched a win, ending one of the greatest rivalries of all time.

After defeating Austin, The Rock focused on electrifying the silver screen. He backed up his previous Hollywood success with lead performances in *Walking Tall* and *Be Cool*. Over seven years, Dwayne "The Rock" Johnson evolved into a mainstream celebrity.

He only made brief appearances in WWE, and the millions (and millions) of WWE fans missed seeing him compete.

However, the same charisma that made him the People's Champ shined through in films.

The Rock in Movies

2019
Fighting with My Family

2018
Rampage

2017
Baywatch
Jumanji

2016
Moana

2015
Furious 7
San Andreas

2014
Hercules

2013
Fast & Furious 6
Empire State

2012
Journey 2:
The Mysterious Island

2011
Fast Five

2010
Tooth Fairy

2009
Race to Witch Mountain

2008
Get Smart

2007
The Game Plan

2005
Be Cool

2004
Walking Tall

2003
The Rundown

2002
The Scorpion King

2001
The Mummy Returns

In February 2011, WWE made a blockbuster announcement. Finally, The Rock was back in WWE! Promising to once again "bring it," he traded insults with WWE's biggest current star, John Cena. At *WrestleMania XXVII*, he dropped the Cenation leader with a Rock Bottom, costing Cena his match.

For over a year, their rivalry became increasingly hostile. At *WrestleMania XXVIII*, in The Rock's hometown of Miami, the stage was finally set for a once in a lifetime clash.

Cena gave The Great One all he could handle. The combatants were equal in strength, skill, and desire. Cena tried to finish The Rock with his own People's Elbow, but The Rock sprang to his feet just in time. He delivered a thunderous Rock Bottom and pinned Cena to win another classic battle of generations.

The Rock vowed to once again become WWE Champion. It had been ten years since he last held the celebrated prize, which was currently around the waist of CM Punk. Known as the "Best in the World," Punk was as dominant as he was brash. For 434 days, no one could beat him for the title.

With his mother in attendance, The Rock faced Punk at *Royal Rumble* 2013. The competitors fought fearlessly. After an ambush  by The Shield nearly derailed the contest, The Rock dug down. He countered Punk move for move, then connected with a People's Elbow for the win. His eighth WWE Championship was the perfect capstone to a miraculous career.

There is no telling what The Rock will do next. He still trains extremely hard, just like his father taught him decades ago. His regimen includes intense weight training and cardio to build strength and stamina. He also follows a strict diet, eating lots of protein and avoiding too many sweets.

The Rock Facts

- The term "SmackDown" was first used by The Rock before it became the title of one of WWE's weekly shows in 1999.

- In college, The Rock shared defensive line duties with NFL legend Warren Sapp.

- The Rock has appeared on several TV shows, including *Saturday Night Live*. He also portrayed his own father in an episode of *That '70s Show*.

- The Rock was Forbes' top grossing actor in 2013. That means people spent more money to see his movies ($1.3 billion dollars!) than any other actor.

With this strong work ethic, The Rock will be ready for whatever challenge lies ahead. You can guarantee that no one—and The Rock means *no one*—will ever lay the smackdown in sports and entertainment quite like Dwayne "The Rock" Johnson.

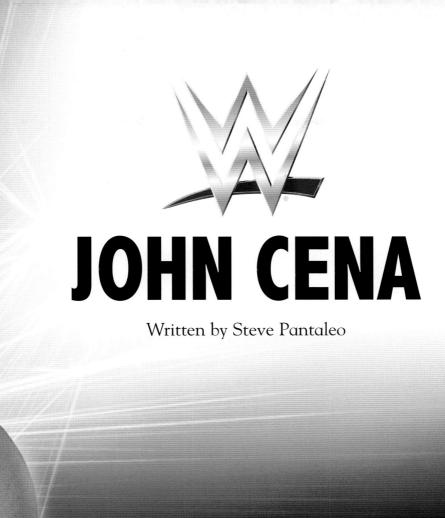

JOHN CENA

Written by Steve Pantaleo

John Cena became a WWE fan when he was a young boy. He sat in front of his television every Saturday morning as Hulk Hogan, Andre the Giant, Ultimate Warrior, and the rest of WWE's Superstars competed in the ring. Their athleticism and colorful personalities caught the young Cena's imagination. He was so captivated that he even created cardboard titles and wore them around the house, pretending to be like the champions he watched on television.

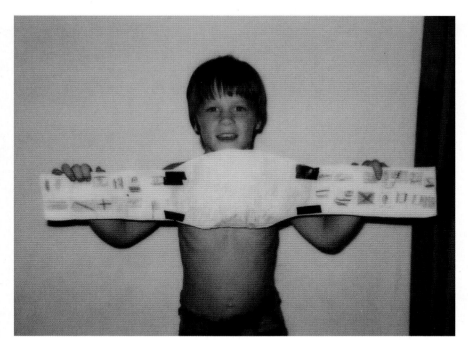

Cena also loved hip-hop music and fashion. He liked to make up his own songs, but they weren't very popular in his hometown of West Newbury, Massachusetts. The other kids in his town listened to hard rock music. They teased Cena for being different.

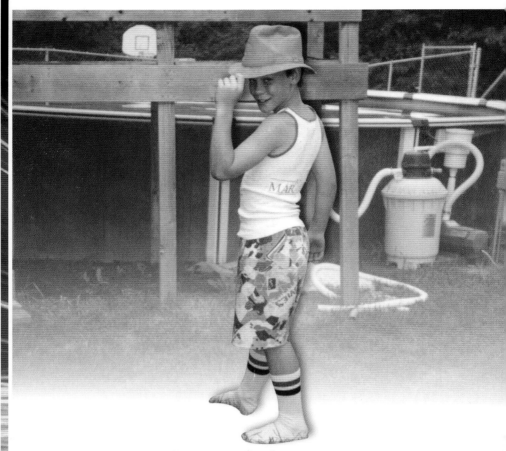

However, Cena didn't pay attention to the kids that teased him. He just kept doing what made him happy.

The teasing finally stopped when Cena started bodybuilding at the age of 15.

The more Cena exercised, the stronger he became. As Cena's muscles got bigger, the other kids stopped picking on him. After high school, Cena went to Springfield College. He was the captain of the football team and earned a degree in exercise physiology.

John Cena Stats

Height: 6' 1"
Weight: 251 lbs.
From: West Newbury,
Massachusetts
Signature Moves:
Attitude Adjustment,
STF

Cena began working at a gym in California after college. While there, he met another bodybuilder who urged him to try to become a WWE Superstar.

Cena liked the idea, but he knew it would be hard work. Hoping to learn the proper way to compete, he enrolled in the Ultimate Pro Wrestling school in 2000.

John Cena Facts

- Nobody has held the WWE Championship more times than John Cena.
- John Cena has won Tag Team Championships with Shawn Michaels, Batista, David Otunga, and The Miz.
- John Cena hosted *Saturday Night Live* in 2016.
- John Cena has more than 5.8 million Twitter followers and 17 million Facebook Likes.

Cena learned very quickly. Within weeks, his training paid off when he won the UPW Heavyweight Championship in April. Soon, WWE officials learned about the young competitor and signed him to a contract. They sent him to Ohio Valley Wrestling to complete his training and learn how to become a WWE Superstar.

Cena became an official WWE
Superstar in June 2002. His first
match was against Kurt Angle.
Cena lost the match, but
showed great determination
and willpower. It was clear
that Cena was going to be
a big star.

The young Cena defeated many top stars over the next few months, including Chris Jericho. He also started to show some of the traits he had while growing up.

Just like he did when he was a boy, Cena began wearing hip-hop clothes and rapping before matches. This time, though, nobody made fun of him. Cena was respected by everybody around him because of his hard work and determination.

By 2004, Cena had become one of WWE's top Superstars. Many fans saw January's *Royal Rumble* as his big chance to earn a WWE Championship Match at *WrestleMania*.

However, Cena's dreams of winning the Rumble Match were crushed when he was thrown over the top rope by Big Show.

Cena gained revenge from Big Show when he defeated the giant.

This won him the United States Championship at *WrestleMania XX*. It was Cena's first of many WWE title wins.

Cena held the U.S. Championship three different times in 2004. During this time, he replaced the traditional title with a new one that featured a spinning American flag in the center.

In 2005, Cena earned a WWE Championship Match against JBL at *WrestleMania 21*. It was the biggest match of Cena's career up to that point. Fans from all over the world watched to see if he really was good enough to beat the reigning champ.

Lesser Superstars would've folded under the pressure of competing on WWE's biggest stage. John Cena didn't. Instead, he proved he was WWE's best when he pinned JBL after delivering an Attitude Adjustment.

Just like his heroes before him, John Cena was WWE Champion. Shortly after the win, Cena once again revealed his own version of the title. This one featured a spinning WWE logo in the center.

Winning the title at *WrestleMania* meant that Cena was the best Superstar in WWE. He was also quickly becoming a huge star outside of WWE. Shortly after becoming champ, Cena released his own rap album called *You Can't See Me.*

The album was a big success. It even debuted at number 15 on the *Billboard* charts.

That's not all.
Cena also
completed the
filming of his
first starring
role in a major motion picture,
The Marine. With so much going
on in and out of the ring, Cena
was becoming one of the biggest
stars in WWE history.

John Cena Movies

- *Bumblebee*
- *Ferdinand*
- *Daddy's Home*
- *The Marine*
- *12 Rounds*
- *Legendary*
- *Fred: The Movie*
- *The Reunion*
- *Scooby-Doo!*
    WrestleManiaMystery

The Marine

Cena's title reign was cut short in January 2006. Edge defeated him for the WWE Championship at *New Year's Revolution*.

Cena didn't let the loss get him
down. Instead, he focused all his
attention on winning back the
gold. Just three short weeks after
the loss, he beat Edge to reclaim
the title.

With the gold
back around his
waist, Cena
defeated some of
WWE's biggest
names, including

Big Show and Randy Orton.
He even used his STF submission to
beat Triple H at *WrestleMania 22.*

The following year at *WrestleMania 23*, he used the same move to beat Triple H's longtime friend Shawn Michaels.

Cena held the WWE Title for more than one year before Randy Orton injured the champ's right pectoral muscle in October 2007. The injury was so severe that Cena needed immediate surgery. He was forced to give up the WWE Championship.

Doctors told Cena he could be out of action for up to one full year. However, after less than four months of grueling rehab, he made a surprise return at the 2008 *Royal Rumble*. He last eliminated Triple H to win the Rumble Match. It was the first of two *Royal Rumble* victories for Cena.

2008
Royal
Rumble

Heading into *Survivor Series* 2008, Cena had already won nearly every major championship there was to win.

However, one major title had eluded him his entire career: The World Heavyweight Championship. That night, Cena defeated Chris Jericho in the main event. He claimed his first of three World Heavyweight Championship reigns.

Cena was the target of a vicious attack by The Nexus in June 2010. Led by Wade Barrett, the renegade group spent the rest of the year trying to prove their superiority over Cena. At one point, Barrett even beat Cena. Because of the loss, Cena was forced to temporarily join The Nexus.

Cena eventually got his revenge on his rivals. He defeated Barrett in a Chairs Match at *WWE TLC* in December 2010. The following month, Cena eliminated many Nexus members from the *Royal Rumble* match. This marked the end of their lengthy rivalry.

Hoping to regain the WWE Championship, Cena challenged The Miz at *WrestleMania XXVII*. Unfortunately, The Rock interfered in the match and landed a Rock Bottom on Cena. From there, The Miz slid in and pinned Cena for the win.

The next night on *Raw*, Cena challenged The Rock to a match. The Rock quickly accepted, and the contest was set for *WrestleMania XXVIII*. This was the very first time that the biggest show of the year's main event was set one full year ahead of time.

Two of the biggest names in WWE history finally collided when Cena and The Rock squared off at

WrestleMania XXVIII. It was one of the biggest matches of all time. When the dust from the dream match cleared, The Rock stood tall as the winner. However, Cena wasn't done with The Rock yet.

After winning the 2013 *Royal Rumble*, Cena chose to battle The Rock once again at *WrestleMania*. This time, the stakes were even higher. The Rock's WWE Championship was on the line. In the end, Cena gained revenge from his previous year's loss. He pinned The Rock to win the WWE Championship.

John Cena has been WWE's top star for over a decade. Every time he  enters an arena, he knows that "Hustle, Loyalty, and Respect" can help him be a champion inside and outside the ring. No matter how down he feels, he's reminded to "Never Give Up." Because of this hard work and dedication, John Cena has become one of the all-time greatest WWE Superstars.

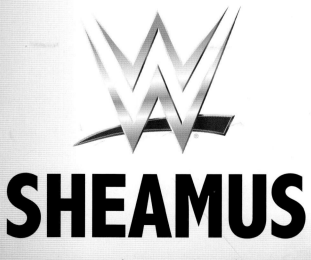

SHEAMUS

Written by Steve Pantaleo

In his impressive career, Sheamus, nicknamed "The Great White," has taken WWE by storm.

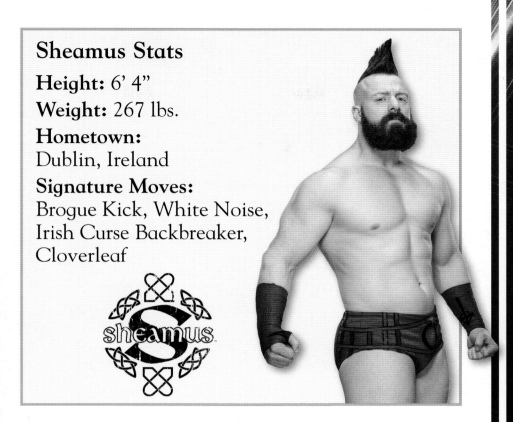

Sheamus Stats

Height: 6' 4"
Weight: 267 lbs.
Hometown:
Dublin, Ireland
Signature Moves:
Brogue Kick, White Noise,
Irish Curse Backbreaker,
Cloverleaf

The first and only Irish-born WWE Champion in history, Sheamus shocked the world by winning the title a mere six months after his WWE debut. For The Celtic Warrior, it was part of a historic quest started centuries ago.

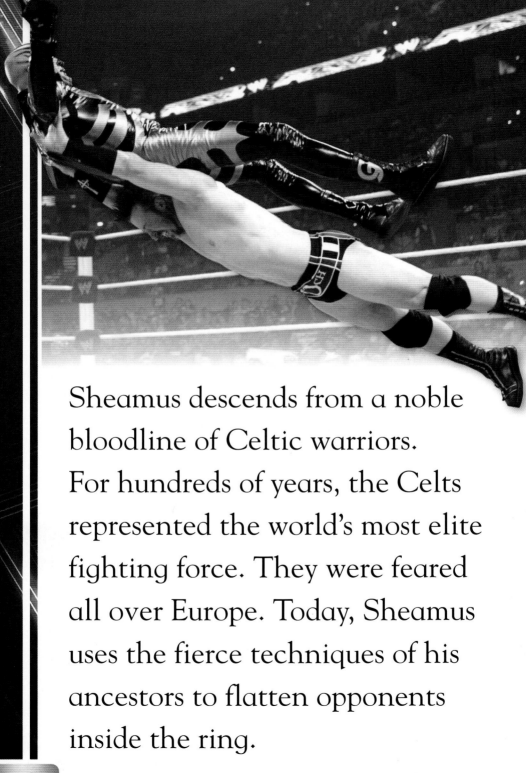

Sheamus descends from a noble bloodline of Celtic warriors. For hundreds of years, the Celts represented the world's most elite fighting force. They were feared all over Europe. Today, Sheamus uses the fierce techniques of his ancestors to flatten opponents inside the ring.

Sheamus first appeared in WWE in June 2009 as part of an effort to bring fresh, new Superstars into the ECW brand. While competing in ECW, he defeated veterans such as Shelton Benjamin and Goldust.

With rippling muscles, milky white skin, and fiery red hair to match his temper, Sheamus stood out from the crowd in ECW. It was not long before he attracted attention from *Monday Night Raw*. In October 2009, he jumped over to WWE's flagship show.

Immediately, Sheamus made his presence felt by pummeling Jamie Noble and announcer Jerry "The King" Lawler. Noble was forced to retire from the damage that Sheamus inflicted. It was clear that this brute Irishman belonged on the big stage.

At *Survivor Series* 2009, Sheamus was a key factor in a five-on-five elimination match. He eliminated two members of the opposition, including team captain John Morrison, to help his team prevail. Sheamus defeated another Irish brawler, Finlay, to earn a spot in a Breakthrough Battle Royal.

Sheamus Signature Moves

Brogue Kick

White Noise

This was set up by Jesse "The Body" Ventura. Any Superstar who had never held a World Championship could enter. A sign of things to come, Sheamus emerged from the crowded pack. The win earned him the right to challenge for the WWE Championship.

Irish Curse Backbreaker

Cloverleaf

Few Superstars in WWE's 50-year history have earned a WWE Championship opportunity in their rookie year. To compound matters, Sheamus would challenge John Cena, WWE's top Superstar. For several years, Cena had dominated WWE. At times, the long-standing champ seemed unbeatable.

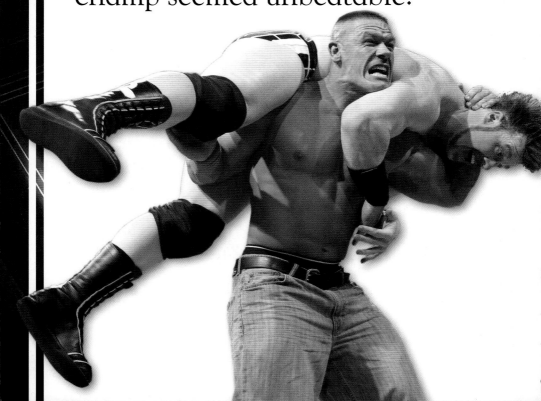

Very few people believed that an
untested Superstar had a chance
against him. Only one man
thought Sheamus would win:
The Celtic Warrior himself.
Sheamus believed that a Tables
Match, where the winner is
the first to throw his opponent
through a table, played right into
his hands.

In a battle for the ages, the two competitors collided with force, trading bone-crushing blows. With Sheamus weary and perched on the top turnbuckle, it appeared the reigning champ would drive his opponent through the timber and claim victory. Instead, Sheamus powered out of Cena's grasp and shoved him crashing through the table below. Sheamus stood victorious with his first WWE Championship. His doubters sat in stunned silence, wondering if anyone could stop this uncontrollable Irishman.

Fastest to First WWE Championship

Champion	WWE Debut	First WWE Championship	Days
Pedro Morales*	11/21/70	2/8/71	79
Ric Flair*	9/9/91	1/19/92	132
Yokozuna*	10/31/92	4/4/93	155
Brock Lesnar	3/18/02	8/25/02	160
Sheamus	**6/30/09**	**12/13/09**	**166**
AJ Styles	1/24/16	9/11/16	231
Kane	10/5/97	6/28/98	266
Big Show	2/14/99	11/14/99	273
Kurt Angle*	11/14/99	10/22/00	343
Alberto Del Rio	8/20/10	8/14/11	359

*WWE Hall of Famer

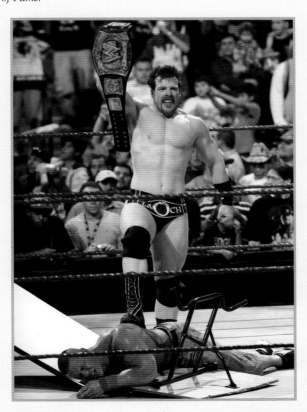

Sheamus was awarded a 2009 Slammy Award for Breakout Superstar of the Year. Although his first reign as WWE Champion was short lived, ending at Elimination Chamber, the Celtic Warrior would not give up.

He quickly turned his attention to the legendary King of Kings, Triple H. The Game would get the best of Sheamus in his first *WrestleMania* match, but he got his revenge weeks later. In a Street Fight at *Extreme Rules*, Sheamus's punishing attacks sidelined Triple H for ten months.

At *Fatal Four Way* in June 2010, Sheamus defeated three top Superstars to reclaim the WWE Championship. Once again,

he beat John Cena and won the gold. The merciless bruiser held the title for three months

before losing it in a Six-Pack Challenge Match at *Night of Champions*. Still, The Great White had yet to be defeated in a one-on-one match for the championship.

Hoping to rebound from the setback, Sheamus set his sights on the 2010 *King of the Ring* tournament. With wins against two of WWE's most athletic stars, Kofi Kingston and John Morrison, Sheamus became the 18th King of the Ring in WWE history.

Though most would think it's good
to be the king, Sheamus soon faced
hardship for the first time.

After more than a year of pushing his fellow Superstars around, Sheamus began to feel the backlash. John Morrison scored a payback win for their *King of the Ring* clash. Then the man he brutally injured ten months earlier, Triple H, inflicted his own brand of punishment on The Great White. Soon, Sheamus found himself on the losing end of matches with the likes of Evan Bourne and future longstanding rival, Daniel Bryan.

When Sheamus
was drafted to
SmackDown in
2011, he seized
the opportunity
for a fresh start.
Seeing the error
of his ways,

he shed his bullish nature for
a more fan-friendly attitude.
Now feeding off the cheers of the
WWE Universe, The Great White
rattled off a winning streak just in
time for the *Royal Rumble*.

The *Royal Rumble* is where the
Road to WrestleMania begins.

If Sheamus could be the last Superstar remaining after twenty-nine others were tossed from the ring, he would be headed to the Show of Shows.

The match included the 425-pound Big Show and the 2009 winner, Randy Orton. However, the end came down to Sheamus and Chris Jericho. Sheamus used a Brogue Kick to knock Y2J over the top rope.

Epic Championship Triumphs

Fatal Four Way Match for the World Heavyweight Championship

Sheamus vs. Alberto Del Rio vs. Chris Jericho vs. Randy Orton

Over the Limit: May 20, 2012

2-out-of-3 Falls Match for the World Heavyweight Championship

Sheamus vs. Daniel Bryan

Extreme Rules: April 29, 2012

Career vs. United States Title Match

Daniel Bryan vs. Sheamus

Monday Night Raw: March 14, 2011

Steel Cage Match for the WWE Championship

Sheamus vs. John Cena

Money in the Bank: July 18, 2010

Tables Match for the WWE Championship

John Cena vs. Sheamus

WWE TLC: Tables, Ladders & Chairs: December 13, 2009

Just like the Breakthrough Battle Royal two years earlier, the powder-skinned powerhouse was the last man standing when the dust settled on the 2012 *Royal Rumble*.

Two months later at *WrestleMania XXVIII*, Sheamus earned his defining victory in WWE. When Daniel Bryan paused to steal a kiss from bombshell AJ Lee, The Great White capitalized.

Sheamus leveled the distracted "Yes Man" with a Brogue Kick, winning the title match in a record eighteen seconds.

The win kicked off an astounding title reign that cemented Sheamus's status as a dominant force in WWE. One month later, he proved his win over Daniel Bryan was not just luck.

In a 2-out-of-3 Falls Match,
Bryan evened the match by
snapping on the Yes! Lock.
Sheamus was weakened, but not
defeated. He summoned all his
determination. After surviving
an onslaught of kicks from Bryan,
the Brogue Kick once again found
its mark. Sheamus earned the
decisive three-count, winning the
grueling match.

As World Heavyweight Champion, Sheamus took on all challengers.

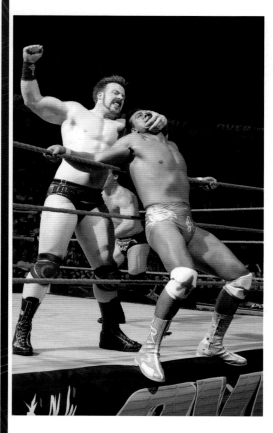

He infuriated Alberto Del Rio by taking his prized car for a joyride. The arrogant aristocrat tried everything to take Sheamus's title, even attempting to have the Brogue Kick banned. Still, Sheamus successfully defended the gold against Del Rio, Dolph Ziggler, and others.

When Big Show finally defeated him at *Hell in a Cell* 2012, Sheamus had been champion for 210 days. Since then, he has joined forces with other Superstars to take on The Shield, while

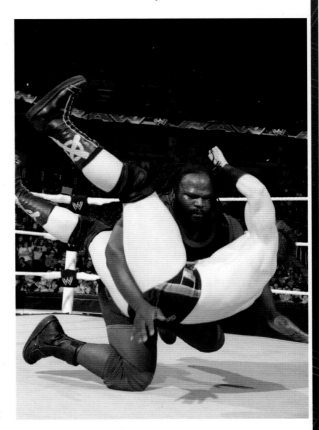

continuing to fight his own battles. He even matched muscle with strongman Mark Henry in a series of strength tests.

Today, Sheamus remains one of the most popular Superstars in WWE. With enough accolades to cement a permanent place in history, his fighting spirit wills him to take on the next challenge. After being injured for much of 2013, the Celtic Warrior came back more aggressive than ever.

Any WWE Superstars on the championship scene had better take notice, because this fella will always be one Brogue Kick away from a 1-2-3.

Sheamus Facts

- The word "Laoch" on Sheamus's ring attire comes from Ireland's native Gaelic language, and means "warrior" or "hero."

- Sheamus's 210-day reign as World Heavyweight Champion is the third longest in WWE history, behind Triple H and Batista.

- In December 2009, Sheamus lived the dream of several NBA referees by putting Dallas Mavericks owner Mark Cuban through a table.

- In the summer of 2013, Sheamus matched wits with Damien Sandow in a series of intellectual challenges, proving he was more than just brawn.

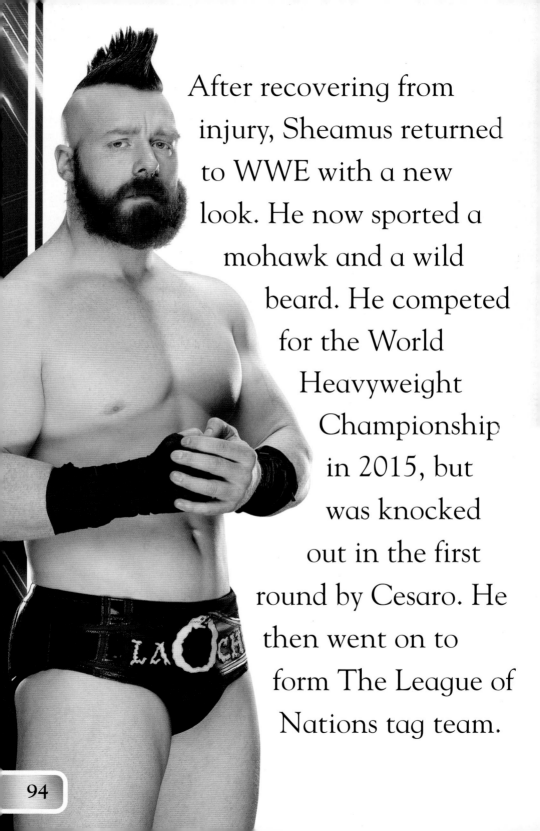

After recovering from injury, Sheamus returned to WWE with a new look. He now sported a mohawk and a wild beard. He competed for the World Heavyweight Championship in 2015, but was knocked out in the first round by Cesaro. He then went on to form The League of Nations tag team.

The League of Nations defeated tag team champions The New Day at *WrestleMania 32* before splitting up. After moving to *RAW*, Sheamus teamed with rival, Cesaro, and they won the *Tag Team Championship* at *Roadblock: End of the Line.*

Glossary

Charisma
A special charm that makes someone popular.

Debut
The first performance of a new wrestler.

Elude
To avoid something or someone.

Excel
To be very good at something.

Grueling
Very difficult and tiring.

Grit
Bravery and strength.

Hostile
Unfriendly and showing that something or someone is not liked.

Veterans
People that have a lot of experience.